BABY LOVE

March 2003

Hope Vestergaard

by Hope Vestergaard

illustrated by John Wallace

DUTTON CHILDREN'S BOOKS • NEW YORK

CIP Data is available.

Published in the United States 2002
by Dutton Children's Books,
a division of Penguin Putnam Books for Young Readers
345 Hudson Street, New York, New York 10014
www.penguinputnam.com

Designed by Alyssa Morris and Irene Vandervoort
Printed in Hong Kong
First Edition
ISBN 0-525-46902-8
1 3 5 7 9 10 8 6 4 2

For Michael
and our lovely babies,
Max and Carsten
— H. Y.

To Tom and Ginger
— J. W.

Baby Love

In all kinds of families
All over the land,
There's one common language we all understand.
The words will come later—
Small cries and sweet coos
Are all babies need now to tell us their news:
I'm hungry!

    I'm tired!

        I love you so much!

They speak with their eyes and they listen to touch.
So go get your baby, come sit for a while—
We'll celebrate all kinds of love, baby-style.

Welcome

Funny faces peeking in,

Sniffing, squeezing softie skin.

Checking fingers, counting toes,

Lining teddies up in rows.

Aunts and uncles,

Grams and Pops . . .

All this peeking never stops.

Cousins, neighbors, paperboy

Come to see my brand-new toy.

Can't Wait

I just can't wait till you get bigger…
Big enough to talk with me:
Tell me all your baby secrets,
Join me for a cup of tea.
I just can't wait till you get bigger…
Big enough to walk with me
Hand in hand along the sidewalk,
Talking 'bout the things we see.

Two of a Kind

Not much hair—
    just like Grandpa.
Love to stare—
    just like Grandpa.
Goofy smile—
    just like Grandpa.
Rest a while . . .
    just like Grandpa.

Breakfast

I will never understand
Why you always use your hands.
Squishy cool and sticky sweet,
This is how you like to eat!
Fruity dribbles on your chin—
Scoop 'em up
And smoosh 'em in.

Bathtime

Bathtime's sloppy in the sink—
Open wide and catch a drink!
Pop the bubbles with your toe,
Water *sloshing* to and fro.
Bubble beard drips down your chin,
Sudsy fingers scrub your skin.
Slippy, slidey, soapy joking—
Why am *I* the one who's soaking?!

Finders Keepers

Here it comes . . .
    There it goes!
What's this bump?
    A baby nose!
What's this flap?
    A floppy ear!
Where is that thing?
    Right over here!
Hey, you caught it!
Don't you know?
You found your hand!
Now don't let go!

Fancy Feet

Two shoes,

New shoes,

Tippy, tappy blue shoes!

See-what-you-can-do shoes:

Do you want to walk?

Cutie Pie

Hats and ribbons, fancy shirts,

Lacy socks and ruffled skirts.

Grown-ups think this stuff is cute . . .

But you prefer your birthday suit!

When You Cry

Sometimes hungry,
Sometimes sad.
Sometimes tired,
Or even glad.
Sometimes just a little wet,
Sometimes quite a bit upset!
Sometimes bored,
Sometimes lonely . . .
Sometimes Mom's your one and only.

Lunch

We are wearing soup for lunch:
Me, a little,
You, a bunch!

Rockabye

In Gram's arms,
    Cozy tight.
In her glasses
    Pictures bright.
In her voice
    Such sweet delight . . .

Oh, how we love to read!
Turn the pages—
    Gentle hands.
Take us places—
    Silly lands.
Grandma always
    Understands
Just how we love to read.

Blankie

He loves your splatters,

Loves your snags,

Loves your tatters and your tags.

Loves your middle,

Loves your sides,

Loves your magic carpet rides!

Where you are:

His favorite spot.

You're his blankie,

He's your tot.

Diapers

Wiggle waggle to and fro...
Sure looks like you want to GO!

The Sandbox

Baby's small.
I am big.
Baby sits
While I dig.

Baby dumps
When I fill.
Baby grabs,
Then I spill.

Baby wrecks,
So I shout.
Baby cries
While I pout.

Baby crawls . . .
I just stare!
Baby hugs . . .
Now we share.

Treats

Keys and crayons,
Chubby feet,
Teething toys,
A doggy treat!
Yummy things to taste and chew—
You want to share?
Uhh . . . no, thank you!

First Tooth

Baby's grumpy,
Down and dumpy!
In those gums
There's something *bumpy*!

His Grace

Baby sits and watches us
From his royal chair.
Snacks on crackers while we work,
Crumb crown in his hair.
Mommy shakes the tablecloth,
Daddy stirs the pots.
I find glasses, forks, and spoons
And set them in their spots.
Baby gets a special spoon,
Bangs it on his cup,
Clangs that silver dinner bell:
Come on, time to sup!
As we sit to give our thanks,
Baby nods and then,
Soon as Mommy's done with grace,
Baby shouts "AMEN!"

Bedtime Boogie

Flick my fingers,

Stomp your feet.

Music in us—feel the beat!

Swing my arms,

Twirl around.

Shake our bottoms,

Touch the ground.

Here comes Mommy . . .

Now's our chance!

Won't you join

Our bedtime dance?

Cozy

Flannel sheets,
Bumper pad,
Pictures of your mom and dad,
Shooting stars
Above your head . . .
Isn't this a cozy bed?

Can't Sleep

It's time for bed! What's all the noise?
I think she's getting louder!
The hall light's on,
And Daddy's gone
To check that little shouter.
But I know what that baby needs—
She's lonely in her bed.
I sing a soft big brother song
And pat her little head.

Nightcap

So warm and sweet and light,
It calms you in the night.
Goes down as smooth as silk—
You sure love Mommy's milk.

Sweet Dreams

Of all the places you can rest,

Your favorite one is Daddy's chest.

You tuck your head beneath his chin,

Feel his breath and smell his skin.

Your cozy perch moves up and down . . .

Up and down . . .

Up and down . . .

Eyelids heavy, not a sound

As you drift off to sleep.

Sleep Tight

All over the planet, the same precious sight:
Babes and their loves snuggle in for the night.
We wrap them in blankets and sing lullabies,
Then stand by their doorways, deciphering cries:
I'm lonely!

    I'm tired!

        I'm falling asleep!

They know we'll stay close till that last little peep.
So spoil those babies with one extra kiss—
They grow up quickly—enjoy this wee bliss.